W9-AUE-096

Two more jobs, and she would have earned forty-five dollars. Surely that would be enough to replace the earrings. Except, they wouldn't be the same ones. She could never really replace the important ones, the ones Grandma Kate had given Mom. Those were gone forever.

Tess sank to her knees and leaned up against her bed. What about praying? Erin's youth pastor said God knew everything about us and saw inside our hearts.

She whispered, "Dear God, Please help me replace those earrings. Please help me think before I act. I can't . . . I can't seem to do anything right. I lost my mom's earrings, and I totally embarrassed myself today in front of my science group with the papier-mâché. When will I do something right? I should probably try to fix this on my own, right? You probably have more important things on your mind, but thanks for listening. Amen."

Secret Sisters: (se'-krit sis'-terz) n. Two friends who choose each other to be everything a real sister should be: loyal and loving. They share with and help each other no matter what!

Secret ❋ Sisters

Twenty-One
Ponies

Sandra Byrd

WATERBROOK
PRESS
COLORADO SPRINGS

Twenty-One Ponies
Published by WaterBrook Press
5446 North Academy Boulevard, Suite 200
Colorado Springs, Colorado 80918
A division of Random House, Inc.

Scriptures in the Secret Sisters series are quoted from the
International Children's Bible, New Century Version,
copyright © 1986, 1988 by Word Publishing,
Nashville, TN 37214. Used by permission.

The characters and events in this book are fictional,
and any resemblance to actual persons or events
is coincidental.

ISBN 1-57856-230-9

Copyright © 1998 by Sandra Byrd

All rights reserved. No part of this book may be reproduced
or transmitted in any form or by any means, electronic or
mechanical, including photocopying or recording, or by any
information storage and retrieval system, without permission
in writing from the publisher.

Printed in the United States of America

1999

3 5 7 9 10 8 6 4

For my husband, Michael,
whom I prize

one

Diamond Earrings

Saturday Afternoon, October 12

"Tess, I wish you wouldn't always wait until the last minute to decide what you're going to wear," her mom said. "I don't have time to run around town looking for a costume, and Erin will be here to pick you up right after dinner."

Steam rose from the gurgling iron as Mrs. Thomas set it down to maneuver the shirt she was pressing into a new position. A large wicker basket overflowing with warm, tumbled laundry rested on the family room floor. Beside the basket sat Tess Thomas, drawing a smiley face on the sole of her running shoe with a blue ballpoint pen.

"I didn't! Look." Tess held up a shriveled black cloth. "This was my costume from last year's fifth-grade dress-up day. But when I washed it, it shrank all up, and the fur fell off. Now what?"

"What will everyone else wear?"

"How am I supposed to know? I've never been to a harvest party at a church before. Maybe they'll all dress up as angels!"

"I doubt it," her mom said, smiling. "Why don't you call Erin to see if she has some ideas?"

"All right." Tess lumbered to her feet and started to walk toward her bedroom. What if she stuck out at this party? Would everyone think it was dumb she was there? Would she embarrass herself? She dialed Erin's number.

"Hello?"

"Hi. It's me."

"Hi. Is everything okay? I mean, are you still coming tonight?" Erin sounded concerned.

"Yeah, I just don't know what to wear. Do you have any ideas?" Tess asked.

"Hmm, I don't know. I had a hard time thinking of something myself. Let's see. . . ." Erin's voice trailed off.

Tess twirled a strand of her hair around her finger, then untwirled it before coiling it up a second time. "Why is everyone dressing up? It's not Halloween yet."

"Well, we wanted a chance to wear costumes because we work at the church kiddie carnival on Halloween, and we don't get to have a party ourselves."

"Maybe I shouldn't come," Tess said. "Maybe everyone will think it's weird I'm there. What if you go off with some other friends and leave me standing all alone not knowing anyone?"

"Don't worry! I won't leave you. Besides, I told you

other people will be there who aren't from my church. Hey, I have a great idea. Why don't you dress up the same as me? We are Secret Sisters, after all. That way we'll be twins tonight, too, even though no one besides you and me will know our secret."

"Okay," Tess said with relief. She rested her chin in her hand, letting her brown hair rain down around the phone. This was better. If they dressed the same, she would feel more like she belonged. This was Erin's church, after all. "What are you wearing?"

"I'm going to be a snowflake. I'm wearing white jeans, a white T-shirt that I glued silver glitter on in a snowflake pattern, and white sneakers. I guess I'll search through my jewelry to see what would look snowflakey."

"Okay," Tess said. "That's sort of funny. I mean, I don't think it has ever snowed in Scottsdale." In fact, the mid-October Arizona sun generally warmed the days to eighty-five degrees.

"True," Erin said with a giggle.

"I think I can find enough stuff for that costume, Sister!" They both broke out in giggles. "I guess I'll see you about quarter to seven?"

"Yep, we'll be there to pick you up."

"Okay. Bye." Tess hung up the phone and walked back into the family room.

"Well?" her mother asked.

"She's going to be a snowflake. We thought it would be cool, since we're Secret Sisters, if we dressed alike."

"What's a Secret Sister?"

"Well, since we both only have brothers, and since we both wish we had a sister, we decided to be Secret Sisters. You know, pretend we are sisters, but not tell anyone. Like my bracelet." Tess held up her right arm so Mom could see the charm bracelet around her wrist. "Erin and I decided to wear them as our private sign of sisterhood. That's why we bought two exactly alike. Anyway, could I borrow one of Dad's white T-shirts? I don't have one."

"What else does this costume involve?" Mrs. Thomas frowned.

"It's easy, Mom. I promise! I'm going to draw a snowflake on the T-shirt with glue, then sprinkle glitter on it. I'll wear my white jeans and sneakers, if I can find the other one, and some jewelry. Do you have any snowy jewelry?"

"Let me think. I do have a glass-bead necklace you could borrow."

"Thanks, Mom. I'll get it after I've finished with the other stuff. Do we have glitter?"

"In the craft box," she said. "Here, catch." She tossed one of Mr. Thomas's white T-shirts from the laundry basket. It landed on Tess's head, draping over her hair like an old woman's scarf. "Cute, Tess. Why don't you wear it like that?" she teased.

"Right, Mom. I'll be in the kitchen gluing my shirt." Tess pulled the shirt off her head and gave her mother a peck on the cheek.

Rummaging through the kitchen drawers, she found the glue, twisted open the cap, and tried to squirt some on her finger. It spluttered before spitting out a few drops. *Empty. Great.* Hoping this wasn't an indication of how the whole night was going to go, Tess left the kitchen in search of a fresh bottle.

Later, after scarfing down her dinner, she raced back into her room to put on her costume. She pulled on her jeans and looked at herself in her oval, full-length mirror. Biting her lip, she stared at her midriff. Chubby. She pulled on her dad's big T-shirt to hide her stomach. Better.

What if all these church people were holy? What if they didn't like Tess because her family didn't go to church? Well, Erin didn't seem too goody-two-shoes. Neither did Janelle, the sixteen-year-old down the street who stayed with Tess and her brother, Tyler, sometimes when their parents were out late. And Janelle went to church every week.

Tess shook out her brown hair, wishing for the thousandth time that it were straight and shiny instead of wavy and coarse. She could pull it back . . . nah. Her ears would stick out.

"Don't forget about the necklace," Mrs. Thomas called from the kitchen. "I'm going to Smitty's for some milk. If I'm not back before you go, have a great time. Dad's in the family room."

"Bye, Mom," Tess called back. She almost had forgotten the necklace. After lacing up her shoes, one of which had been stuffed under her bed, Tess headed for her mother's jewelry box.

"Wow, I'd forgotten Mom had so much great stuff!" Tess marveled as she pulled out one small drawer after another. She supposed, if she were as old as Mom, she would have collected a lot, too. Finding the glass-bead necklace, Tess clasped it around her neck and stared into the mirror. There. That looked good.

But was it good enough? Tess wanted to make the best impression possible on Erin's friends. She didn't want Erin to be embarrassed or sorry she had brought Tess. What could she wear that would be fantastic? A bracelet maybe?

Tess explored the contents of the other drawers and discovered a small box. "What's in here?" Stroking the soft, midnight velvet, she pried up the lid. The hinges worked noiselessly, and as the box opened, Tess gasped. "Mom's wedding earrings!"

The diamond studs glittered like stars in a moonless sky, capturing stray light and then projecting it into a rainbow burst of radiance. Tess knew that these earrings were her mother's most prized possession after her wedding ring and that Grandma Kate had given them to Tess's mother on her wedding day. Tess also knew her mother was saving them for Tess to wear at her wedding.

"I'll just slip them onto my ears for a minute, to see what they look like." Impulsively, she clasped them on and pulled back her hair, just a teeny bit, before glancing into the mirror. The earrings winked at her, gleaming against Tess's chestnut hair. They were beautiful and sophisticated and made Tess feel that way, too.

"What if I borrowed them? They will be mine, after all, and Mom isn't home to ask. I can slip them right back in the box later tonight." Tess stared at her reflection, liking what she saw. She unclasped them and slipped them into her jeans pocket, planning to sneak them on in the car. As she closed the velvet box, the lid snapped loudly, like an angry turtle whose eggs had been stolen.

"Don't worry," Tess reassured. "I'll bring them home safe and sound."

two

The Heart
of the Matter

Saturday Evening, October 12

"Hi! Here, I'll squash over so you have more room." Erin moved to the middle of the backseat, smashing her brother against the opposite door to make room for Tess.

"Hey!" Erin's brother Tom said. "Give me a little room, if you don't mind. I guess I'll move way to the back."

"No, you won't. You know the back doesn't have a seat belt," Mrs. Janssen answered. "Hi, Tess." She smiled at Tess in the rearview mirror. "I'm glad you could come tonight."

"Me, too," Tess answered. "Thanks for the ride."

"Joshua, please turn down that radio," Mrs. Janssen said to her eight-year-old son riding beside her. "I know it's your turn in the front, but you don't need to blast us all out of the car."

"Okay, Mom. After this song," Josh answered, and his mom nodded her consent.

"Your costume looks almost the same as mine," Erin said, elbowing Tess lightly. "Can you believe what I found?" She motioned to her ears with the back of her hand, jiggling some snowflake earrings.

"Great! They're perfect. Oh, I almost forgot." Tess pulled her hair away from her face and slipped on the glistening earrings.

Erin's jaw dropped. "Are those real?"

"Yep," Tess answered. "They were a wedding gift from my grandma to my mom."

"That's so cool of your mom to let you borrow them! They're gorgeous."

Tess lowered her voice. "Well, she didn't exactly let me borrow them. But she didn't say no, either. She went to Smitty's for milk, and I just borrowed them on my own. I'll put them back tonight. They'll be mine someday, anyway."

Erin crossed one skinny leg over the other, tugging at her blonde French braid before whispering in Tess's ear, "Well, they are pretty. I hope you're right. My mom would be furious."

Tess elbowed her, giggling uncomfortably.

"What's so funny?" Tom asked. His straw-colored hair framed his cornflower-blue eyes. As Tess studied him, she felt certain she had never seen anyone with such cute dimples.

"Nothing," Erin answered as they pulled up to the

church. Tess's stomach churned as she saw swarms of kids outside the building. They all seemed to know one another.

"Come on, Tess." Erin nudged her out of the car. "Let's go."

"I'll be here at nine-thirty sharp," said Mrs. Janssen.

"Okay," Tom and Erin replied in unison. Tom saw his friends and walked over to meet them. Erin pulled Tess inside. "Let's go meet some of my friends."

Large tables draped with pumpkin- and cranberry-colored cloths lined the back wall of the auditorium, while red and gold autumn leaves decorated the rest of the room. On the tables sat half-empty platters of cookies and chips. Large silver bowls held sparkling punch.

Later, after the activities, when everyone sat down for the program, used cups, some half-full, stood at lonely attention here and there on the tables. Tess and Erin perched on chairs near the front as a big, bearded man strummed a guitar on the stage. Everyone sang along—except Tess. "I don't know any of the words," she whispered in Erin's ear.

"That's okay. Just move your mouth and fake it," Erin whispered back. "Look around. No one's watching you anyway."

Tess scanned the room. Erin was right; no one was looking at her. Feeling safer, Tess mouthed some of the words after hearing the chorus sung a few times. The sweet and sour smells of the room—sweat mixed with perfume, vinyl seats, and sweet treats—tickled her nose. She glanced down at the plastic flag in her hand. The group had just finished playing Capture the Glow-in-the-Dark Flag. Tess's team had won, and her team-mates had given her the flag since she was a visitor. This night was turning out all right. Some people wore pretty cool costumes. One person was dressed as a bag of M&M's, and someone else was the Lion from Narnia. Tom was an NBA player, of course.

Tess tugged at her ears again, making sure the earrings were still secure. They were; she would feel better when they were back in the box at home. Why had she ever thought wearing them was a good idea?

"Hey, wake up!" Erin bumped Tess with her elbow.

Tess bumped her back and smiled.

The bearded man left the stage, and the lights dimmed. *Another game?* Tess wondered. But then a man walked onto the stage dressed as a skeleton. You could see his bones and organs, which were cut from glow-in-the-dark plastic. The room grew silent as they waited to see what the skeleton would say.

"Catch!" he called. Velcro ripped as he tore off a fake lung and threw it to the crowd. The girls shrieked, try-ing to avoid the flying lung, but the guys roared and dove for it like fans scrambling for a stray baseball. "Catch!" he called again and threw another lung, then the liver.

The room swelled with laughter as he un-Velcroed his stomach and tossed it to the crowd, then his intestines. The girl next to Erin squealed and shrank back as the large, squishy tube of intestine landed at her feet. She pinched it between thumb and forefinger, tossing it back over her shoulder.

Tess laughed aloud, enjoying herself. This was church? She had to admit, it was fun. The man ripped off his heart and tossed it into the crowd. Tess watched as a familiar hand reached up and plucked it from the air. Tom.

After several minutes of wild laughter and gut tossing, the skeleton took off his mask, leaving only his body costume. "Okay, guys, settle down," he said.

"Who is that?" Tess asked.

"Our youth pastor, Jack. He's crazy," Erin said proudly.

"What's he doing?"

"I don't know, but we're sure to find out soon."

"Okay, I know this gut throwing is a lot of fun, but I actually have a reason for it all," Jack continued as the crowd calmed down a bit. "Who can guess what the most important part of my costume is?"

"The part that covered your face. Put it back on, please!" someone called out from the crowd. The room was roaring with laughter once again, and Jack had to whistle into the microphone to calm down the crowd.

"Okay, guys, get a hold of yourselves here. I really

want an answer," Jack said with a smile. "What part? What part is most important to God?"

"The heart," a girl called from a couple of rows behind Tess.

"You're right!" Jack answered. "Who has the heart?"

Tess turned to look where she knew Tom sat.

"Bring it up, please, Tom."

Tom looked flustered but walked toward the front. He handed the heart to Jack before hurrying back to his seat. "Giving your heart away again, huh, Tom?" Jack teased from the stage.

Tess wished Tom would give her his heart. The thought sounded so loud in her head that she turned to see if Erin had heard it, but Erin watched Jack. Tess turned to watch him, too.

Jack stuck the big, red heart back onto his costume. "Okay, now you have a good picture of what God sees when he looks at us. He sees us from the inside out. He's not looking at how expensive your clothes are, how many zits you have, whether you are popular, or if you're the smartest kid in your class. He's concerned with your heart. And there's no way to hide it from him. It's right there, up front, like it is on me."

Tess stared at the costume. Yep, the heart was pretty plain and clear.

"If you are kind, honest, caring, and pure, God sees that. But none of us can always be like that. Not even me!" He smiled. "God also sees the sin in our hearts.

Doing bad things, anger, jealousy. There's no hiding any of it."

Tess shuddered a bit when Jack said "doing bad things." She guessed she had done something bad to her mother by taking the earrings. And God saw that.

Jack pointed at his costume. "Next time you're out at the store, or at school, or walking down your street, and you see skeleton Halloween decorations, remember that God cares about what is in your heart. He sees you from the inside out and loves you. Ask yourself, 'What is in my heart right now? Is it clean?' If not, ask Jesus to help you make it right. Okay, you guys, let's have the guts!"

People with the lungs, liver, stomach, and other organs rushed forward and reattached them to Jack. Tess watched, catching Jack's eye. He smiled at her, and she blushed, wondering if he could possibly have guessed about the earrings.

As he turned away, she stood up. "We had better go, Erin. Your mom will be waiting."

"Yeah, you're right," Erin answered.

They walked toward the door and stepped out into the cool autumn evening. A breeze caressed Tess's cheek, lifting her heavy hair slightly and blowing a cool breath on her sweaty neck. She stood by the curb and unclasped her mother's diamonds, slipping them into her T-shirt pocket right before Erin's mother pulled up. Erin jumped in and scooted over so Tess would fit in the middle. Tess slid over, making room for Tom. A happy ending to a nice night.

"Did you enjoy yourselves?" Erin's mother asked.

"Yeah, it was great. Jack threw his guts at us," Tom said enthusiastically.

"What?" Erin's mom glanced back at them in the rearview mirror as she took off.

"It's a long story, Mom," Erin answered. She settled back into her seat. "Did you have a good time?" she whispered to Tess.

"Yeah, I really did." Tess whispered back, smiling.

"Do you want to come with me to church tomorrow?"

"No, I'm hiking with my dad." Tess started to feel cramped in the backseat, hot and uncomfortable. "He couldn't go last Thursday night so we're going tomorrow. Thanks anyway."

"Okay," Erin said. They talked about everything that had happened that night, especially what costumes people wore, until they pulled up to Tess's front door.

three

Something Terrible

Saturday Night, October 12

"Hi, guys. I'm home," Tess called down the hall as she slammed the front door on the night behind her.

"We're in the family room, honey," her mom called back. "Come on down and tell us about the party."

Tess's eyes shone, and her cheeks were pink with excitement. "I had a great time. Look!" She proudly held up the plastic flag. "We played Capture the Glow-in-the-Dark Flag, which was totally fun. And they gave me the flag since I was visiting!" She kicked off her sneakers and sat down next to her dad.

"Did you know anyone besides Erin?" her dad asked.

"No, but it was okay. I met the people on my flag team, and we did a lot of stuff in groups. So I didn't feel weird or anything. This guy dressed up like a skeleton and talked about God seeing our hearts. It gave me a lot to think about. I might like to go back sometime." Tess caught a look her dad gave her mother. "Is that okay?"

"We'll see. You had better get to bed so you're ready to hike tomorrow morning." Mr. Thomas ruffled her hair as he stood up. "I'm going to drink a glass of water and then head for bed myself."

A minute later Tess heard him open the freezer door and then the ice tinkled as it dropped into his glass.

"I'm glad you had a good time, honey," her mother said. "I went to church a bit when I was a girl, but after my dad died, we gradually stopped going. I don't know why. I never asked my mom. I guess we were busy with other things." Molly Thomas looked out beyond Tess, talking more to herself than to her daughter.

Then she focused on Tess again. "Well, off to bed. I'm going to finish cleaning the kitchen, then I'm hitting the hay, too."

Tess kissed her mom good night and headed down the hall toward her bedroom. Stopping at the door just before hers, she knocked.

"Tyler?" she called softly. There was no answer. She opened the door a crack and saw eight-year-old Tyler asleep, with his head at the foot of the bed, walkie-talkie still in his hand. She tiptoed in and took the walkie-talkie, covered him with the blanket, and patted his mussed brown hair. "You're okay, I guess, even if you can be a pest."

She glanced over at Hercules, Tyler's pet horned toad. Hercules stirred and threw himself against the side of his glass cage. "Gross!" Tess said. "You are repulsive." Sneaking out backward, she shut the door and walked into her own room.

As she flicked on the light, she reached her hand into her shirt pocket. "Better put these back in Mom's box before Dad goes to bed," she said to herself.

Wait a minute. She felt around in her seemingly empty pocket. "Maybe I put them in my pants pocket," she mumbled, a little panicked now. Grasping hold of each jeans pocket, she pulled them inside out, sure now that they were empty, too. Fear crawled over her like a thousand ants. She stumbled to the phone, hands shaking as she dialed Erin's number.

"Hello?" came a voice on the other end.

"Erin, something terrible! I can't find my mother's earrings."

"Are you sure?"

"Of course I'm sure! Do you think they could have fallen out in your car?"

"Maybe. I'll check. Hold on." Erin set down the phone and went to go look.

"Please, God," Tess prayed quietly, "I really am sorry I borrowed those earrings without asking. I'm not just saying that, either. I thought that at the party, too. But now I am going to be totally, totally dead if they are lost. And worse yet, my mom will freak out. Please let them be in the car!" Tess heard Erin pick up the phone again.

"I'm sorry, Tess, I couldn't find them. I looked every-where. I'll put up a note at church tomorrow. Whoever finds them can call me."

"I am going to be in so much trouble!" Tess started to cry softly.

"Maybe you should tell your mom," Erin suggested.

"I can't. I have to find them; they mean so much to her."

"I'll pray for you, Tess. I have to go. My dad will be calling for a ride home from the restaurant soon."

"Good night," Tess whispered before hanging up the phone. She turned on her computer and logged on with shaking hands.

Dear Diary,

A major disaster! I borrowed my mom's wedding earrings so I would feel really special tonight, instead of dumb. But I lost them! I checked all my pockets, and they aren't there. Erin even checked her car, but they weren't there either. I know I was wrong, like Jack said, to take them, but I didn't think I'd lose them. My mom will be really mad at me. Maybe she won't trust me anymore. My dad will be really disappointed. Maybe he won't want me to hike the Rim-to-Rim with him in May. Remember? That's when we're going to hike across the Grand Canyon together. What should I do, Diary? Why am I asking you? You're just a diary. I guess I am dumb after all. Impulsive, like my mom says.

Love, Tess

four

No Peace

Sunday, October 13

"You're lagging today. What's the matter?" Mr. Thomas waited as Tess came around the bend and caught up with him. A painfully blue Arizona sky glared down on them, the kind of sky that provided no wisp of cloud to cast a shadow, no relief from the brightness.

"I, I don't feel good. Could we sit down for a minute?" Tess hobbled over to a flat patch on the side of the path to sit down. Pulling her knees close to her stomach, she clasped her arms around her legs and said, "I have a stomachache."

"Let's rest for a minute," Dad said. "Maybe you'll feel better after you catch your breath. Are you winded?"

"No, I don't think so."

"Well, we can't let up on training if we still want to hike the Rim-to-Rim together in May. Hiking across the Grand Canyon takes stamina, and you're going to have to build it up." Dad stared at Tess's face, and his tone of voice changed. "Your face looks chalky. No one does her best when she's sick. Do you want to go home?"

"I'm not sure. Can we sit here for a minute?" Resting her chin on her knees, Tess glanced around her. A cholla cactus sprang its spindly sticks out of a lump of brown earth, jumping from the bare landscape like the hair sprouting from an old man's mole. No matter how hard she tried, Tess couldn't forget about the diamond earrings or stop worrying about how she would get them back. She knew her dad was counting on her to finish the hike, but her head throbbed and her stomach flip-flopped inside. "I think we should go, Dad. Maybe I'll feel better when we hike Thursday night."

"Okay, honey. Let's walk down." Tess's father put his arm around her, guiding her slowly down the mountain. "Is everything else all right? Did anyone make fun of you last night at that church?"

"No, I had a great time," Tess said. "It's just, well, I don't know . . ." Her voice trailed off.

"It's okay. Tell you what: I have to shower because I have a meeting this morning. We can run home, and while I wash up, you and Mom can buy a Sunday paper and bagels. Tyler can make the juice. Maybe a good brunch will quiet your stomach."

"Okay, Dad." Tess loved bagels. Maybe that would help her think of a plan. She was sure something would come to her.

❋

Later, the tires squealed as her mother gunned the engine and they pulled out of the driveway. For the thousandth time, Tess wondered how such a mild-mannered person could be such a crazy driver. Glad that she still had on her baseball cap from hiking, Tess pulled the bill down lower over her face to hide her embarrassment.

"Are you sure you're feeling okay? Dad said you couldn't finish the hike. Let me see your face."

Tess pulled the cap back up so her mom could look at her. "I'm fine, Mom, really," she insisted. "It's just a stomachache."

"You've had a lot of stomachaches this year. And your color is not good. Could you have eaten anything bad last night?"

"No, I don't think so." Uncomfortable about keeping the secret of the lost earrings from her mother, Tess changed the subject. "I love bagels. This is a great treat. Can we have flavored cream cheese? Can I order a blueberry bagel?"

"Sure. Tyler wants cinnamon-raisin, Dad wants two with garlic. I'm not sure what flavor I want yet. I'll see what looks good when we get there."

A few minutes later Mom jerked the car into Bernie's parking lot. Holding the shop door open for her mother, Tess glanced at the cut-outs of New York sky-scrapers that papered the deli's walls. A large stack of the *New York Times* newspaper lay on the counter, dwarfing the small pile of *Arizona Republics,* the local paper. The room was foggy with the warm mist of freshly baked goods while huge wire baskets held stacks of fresh bagels. There must have been thirty kinds to choose from. Exotic fish, such as smoked whitefish, shone from behind a polished glass case, their dead eyes staring blankly at Tess, as if she could help them.

Trying as hard as she could not to glance at the meats, Tess wandered down to pick up one of the *Arizona Republics*. Curiosity won. She glanced in the deli case to see if Bernie, the deli's owner, was still selling the disgusting thing. He was. A large, pickled cow's tongue, looking like a human's but five times bigger, with giant taste buds, seemed to be licking toward the sky. It still had green clover stains on the surface, so it must have been a new one. Tess had refused to believe people sliced cow's tongue to put it in a sandwich, but Bernie said they did. Gross.

After Mrs. Thomas paid for the bagels, they walked back to the car. Mom revved the engine, and they were off. Just as they rounded the corner to their housing development, a car ahead of them slammed on its brakes. A dog had run into the street. Mrs. Thomas quickly applied her brakes, but because she had been following too closely, they came within inches of slamming into the first vehicle. Tess's head was thrown forward, and she found herself staring at the bumper sticker on the car ahead of her. It read, "Know Jesus, Know Peace. No Jesus, No Peace."

"Are you okay?" her mom asked in a shaken voice.

"Yes, I'm okay." Tess said. They took off again and were soon home.

Tess hardly noticed. She was still thinking about the bumper sticker.

Munching her bagel as she read the comics, Tess didn't hear Tyler until he called loudly, "Hey! Are you listening? Check this out!" His eyes lit up as he passed a part of the paper to Tess. She read the ad announcing that the circus was coming to town.

Tess figured there would be no circus for her after her mom and dad found out about the earrings. As she stared at the paper, her eyes lost focus. She imagined it read, "Introducing our new flying trapeze artist, Tess Thomas, age almost twelve, who had to run away and join the circus after being banished for losing family jewels." Snapping back into reality, Tess blinked and figured she had better stay focused. Her family wouldn't send her away.

"Great, Ty. Why don't you ask Mom if you can go?" she said, handing the paper back.

"I already entered Robinsons' contest to win tickets. I'm sure I'll win!" Tyler raced into the kitchen to show the ad to his mom. Maybe if he won four tickets they would let her go anyway.

She stuffed the last piece of bagel into her mouth and sifted through the paper, searching for an article to clip out for her current events assignment. A headline caught her attention, "Police crack down on child labor ring, preteens caught in sweatshop." Well, at least they were earning money.

Hey, maybe that was an idea. She could find a job and buy her mom a new pair of earrings. Tess had no idea how much they cost, but she was sure it couldn't be too much. It seemed like a good idea, but she didn't feel any less anxious. No peace. Oh well, maybe she would be okay once she purchased the new pair. Even better, maybe someone had found them at Erin's church today. She cut out the article and folded the paper before going to call Erin.

five

Get a Job

Monday, October 14

"Hi," Tess greeted Erin as soon as Erin walked into the classroom. "I tried to call you all day and night yesterday! Your phone was busy. Is everything okay?"

"Yeah," Erin said. "Sometimes my dog knocks the phone off the hook, and we don't realize it. How was the rest of your weekend?" She looked at Tess hopefully.

"Terrible, of course. Unless you're going to tell me someone turned in the earrings yesterday at your church."

"Sorry, they didn't. My mom left a note in the church office; so if anyone finds them, that person can call us." Then Erin said cheerfully, "A lot of people asked if you were coming back to church with me. A couple of the girls on your Capture-the-Flag team said they liked getting to know you and wondered if you were coming back."

Tess said, "Yeah, I'd like to. I'm not sure when. That is, if I'm not killed when Mom and Dad find out I've lost the earrings! What am I going to do?"

"I wish I could help you. Let's think about it and talk more at lunch." Erin turned to face the front as Ms. Martinez, their sixth-grade teacher, came in. Her perfume lightly scented the classroom as she walked to her desk. Both girls liked Ms. M. She was young and listened to what her students said. Not that you had to be young for that.

"I hope you all had a really great weekend. I did!" Ms. M. said with a smile. Her pen worked back and forth across her notepad as she took attendance before continuing. "We'll get to current events in a minute, but first I want to give you your writing assignment for next week. I want each of you to write a fairy tale, fable, or story. You can write an original one, or you may rewrite one you have heard. It needs to be at least two pages long. The emphasis should be on the creative aspect of writing and storytelling, not on fact-finding and reporting. Each of you will stand to read your story aloud in class next Thursday. You will be graded on how entertaining the story is, how you interpret the story's message, and elocution."

Scott Shearin's hand shot up. "What's elocution?"

"Elocution refers to how well you are able to read the story aloud," Ms. M. said with a smile. "I think it will be an entertaining day. I'll bring popcorn and juice, and we'll listen to the stories all afternoon. Now, please take out your current events articles, and we'll discuss a few of them. Joann, would you please read yours?"

Tess turned to Erin, rolling her eyes. Joann was a know-it-all. Her report was sure to be on the stock market, which, of course, Joann's daddy knew all about. Then Joann would follow the article with a lecture. Tess could never understand why Ms. M. called on Joann at all. She seemed to actually like Joann!

Tess pulled out a pen and ripped a scrap of paper off her article. She wrote, "My article gave me an idea. How about if I find a job and make enough money to buy a new pair of earrings for my mom?"

She rolled the scrap into a skinny cylinder, leaned way over toward Erin's desk, and dropped it in her outstretched palm.

After reading the note, Erin answered, "Where are you going to get all that money? How much do they cost?"

She passed the note back to Tess.

Tess read it and answered, "I don't know. Let's talk about it at lunch."

She passed the note back to Erin just as Joann finished reading.

Once they were seated in the school cafeteria, Erin poured so much hot sauce on her taco it ran out the corners. The crispy corn shell crunched noisily when Erin took a bite. "So how are you planning to earn the money?" she asked.

"Well, a neighbor lady called me last night to see if I

can baby-sit Thursday. I'm really excited. And I think it's for three times."

"You baby-sit?" Erin asked.

"Well, I'm just starting. And my mom says only in the afternoon and for older kids."

"Why don't you tell your mom, Tess?" Erin said before taking another bite. The shell shattered so she scooped up the rest with her fork, holding it together with a blob of sour cream.

"I—I can't."

"Your mom seems nice. She'll be mad, but it's better than keeping a secret. I feel sick when I have a secret. Except a good one that doesn't hurt anyone, like being Secret Sisters," Erin said.

"Actually, I was pretty sick on Sunday," Tess admitted. "And I'm still jittery all the time. But I want to try to fix it myself. Will you come to the mall with me? We can look at earrings to see how much they cost."

"Sure. When?"

"How about Friday after school? I'll ask my mom if she'll drive us; then I'll let you know tomorrow."

"What if your mom finds out about the earrings first?" Erin said.

"I don't think she will. She hardly ever wears that pair."

"Okay. Hey, what are you going to do about the writing assignment?" Erin asked.

"Oh, I'll write a story. My mom is a writer, you know,"

Tess said proudly. "I guess I must have some of her genes!"

"I'll rewrite one," Erin said glumly. "I'm not smart. I couldn't think up a new story."

"Why do you always say you're not smart?" Tess demanded.

"Because I'm not. I hardly ever get called on, and I've never gotten an A."

"I'll help you, if you want," Tess said.

"Sure. Okay." Erin didn't look too sure or too okay. "Let's go outside."

As they left the cafeteria, Erin asked, "What do you think is up with Ms. M?"

"Well," Tess said, "I did notice a ring on her fourth finger . . ."

"You're kidding! Do you think she got engaged over the weekend?"

"Maybe," Tess answered. "She said she had had a really great weekend."

"Dreamy," Erin said. "Should we ask her?"

"Maybe. Let's see if the time is right," Tess said. Talking about weddings reminded her of the lost earrings. She wanted to think about something else, anything else.

Later that evening Tess was in her room reading when her mom knocked on the door. "Could you please come out to help Tyler set the table for dinner?"

"Sure, Mom," Tess said. They headed back to the

kitchen together. "Hey, where's Mrs. Kim's phone number? I guess I'll call her back and tell her I'll baby-sit Thursday."

Her mom glanced at her with surprise. "Why the sudden change of heart?"

"Oh, I'm saving money for something," Tess answered, hoping her mother wouldn't press her for details.

Mrs. Thomas walked to the small desk in the kitchen and handed Tess a piece of note paper. "Here's the number. Help Tyler first, though," Mom said.

Tess opened the cupboard where the glasses were kept and took out four plastic ones. She set the blue one at her place, but Tyler yelped, "Blimey! I say, my turn for the blue glass."

"No, 'fraid not, Inspector," Tess answered. Tyler spoke with a British accent half the time—when he remembered, that is. He watched and taped the British mystery shows that played on PBS each week.

"Listen, old girl, give it to me!" Tyler grabbed the glass, and the two of them struggled over it.

"Hey! Calm down, you two! It's not like that glass is the most valuable thing in the world," said her mom.

No, the wedding earrings probably are, Tess thought.

six

Ready to Explode

Thursday, October 17

"Okay, sixth graders, please pair up with your science partner. Each pair will join with other groups so we have teams of eight people, each working on a particular part of the Mount Vesuvius project. Remember, the winning class gets to go to the planetarium, so let's all pull together to do our best!" Ms. M. signaled for everyone to move to the science tables in a corner of the classroom.

Tess and Erin grouped together with six others. The rest of the class divided up, too. Ms. M. handed out instruction cards for each team. Joann grabbed the card for their group; she always made sure she was the project leader.

"Okay, you guys, our job is to build the actual volcano," Joann announced. "Could someone get the sack of papier-mâché?" All Joann needed was a clipboard, a whistle, and a cap, and she would be the perfect coach.

41

After she had turned her back, Jim saluted her before going to the cupboard for the papier-mâché. Tess giggled. She thought Joann was bossy, too.

"I'll get the water," Erin volunteered. Grabbing a plastic watering can, she headed for the drinking fountain. As she left the table, she bumped into Scott Shearin. "Oh, sorry," she said, blushing.

"What should I do?" Tess asked their coach.

"Empty the shredded newspaper into the bowl," Joann answered.

Tess struggled to open the bag, but the plastic was thick. "Does anyone have scissors?" she asked. All the team members shook their heads. "Oh, all right," Tess said, as she ripped open the bag with her teeth. She tore a bit too much, and shredded newspaper spewed from the bag and into her mouth, coating her teeth with the dry, earthy scraps.

"Ha-ha, look, Tess can't wait for lunch!" Scott pointed at her.

"Very funny!" Tess said, wiping the newsprint out of her mouth with quick, embarrassed swipes.

Joann delegated the tasks, and soon they were building their volcano. One person placed the lava ingredients into the test tube, another built the mountain base, and Tess mashed together the shredded paper with her hands. It felt like slippery, wet gum but gritty, too, like gum that had been dropped on the beach. Erin came to help her.

"Are you baby-sitting those kids today?" she asked.

"I guess so," Tess answered.

"Yeah, well, at least it's money!"

"They aren't too bad, actually. I hope I'll make enough to buy my mom new earrings. Or at least get enough for a down payment!" The goop on Tess's fingers started to harden, and she hurried to sculpt the mountain. She left a small hole at the top for the eruption. Looking at the volcano, she thought how it represented her right now—churning on the inside, sick with pressure, ready to explode. "I hope we can find some new earrings tomorrow," she said uneasily.

"Me, too," Erin said. "What time will you be by to pick me up?"

"I don't know. I'll call you after baby-sitting to let you know."

"Okay."

"Come on, you two," Joann barked. "Pay attention; don't you want to win?"

Erin rolled her eyes at Tess before getting back to work.

"Did you ask Ms. M. about her ring?" Erin whispered.

"What ring?" Joann joined the conversation even though she wasn't invited.

Tess glanced at Erin before answering. "We noticed Ms. Martinez had a new ring on her left hand, fourth finger, you know?"

"Oh," Joann said. "So?"

"Well, we think it's sort of romantic and everything,"

Erin said. "I wonder if she's really engaged. And who her fiancé is. Tess, you go ask her. You're brave."

"What's so good about getting married?" Joann muttered. "It's a stupid idea, if you ask me. It never turns out. Let's get back to our project."

Tess looked over at Erin, who raised her eyebrows. They silently returned to their work.

Later that afternoon Tess went over to the Kims' home to baby-sit. "I do appreciate your coming over," Mrs. Kim said. "I'm sure you'll have a fun time with the boys. After all, you have lots of experience with your own brother!" She smiled as she closed the front door, locking Tess in the jail cell with the two boys.

"Okay, guys, what do you want to do, play some games?" Although Tess grumbled, she enjoyed kids, even active ones like Jerry and Joe. As long as they didn't act up.

"No, we want to make a snack," Jerry said.

"Okay," Tess said. "Let's go into the kitchen." They walked from the front hallway into the kitchen.

This was Tess's first baby-sitting job for pay, but she wasn't nervous. She had helped out with Tyler ever since he was born, and she was always in charge of the kids at the family reunion.

"How about a peanut butter and jelly sandwich?" Joe suggested.

"Sure," Tess said. "You guys get the stuff out while I go to the bathroom."

She raced down the hall as quickly as she could, not

wanting to leave them alone for too long. A minute or two later, on her way back down the hallway, she heard giggling from the kitchen. Picking up her pace, she gasped as she entered the room. Blobs of peanut butter covered the beautiful wallpaper of Mrs. Kim's neat kitchen. Joe loaded another blob into his spoon, which he was using as a slingshot, ready to fire another round.

Tess stepped into the room and cried out, "Stop! What are you doing?"

"Nothing," Jerry answered. Then he yelped as Joe nailed him with the blob.

"Okay, you two, cut it out right away, or I'll call your dad at work."

The boys sobered up.

"Now, we have to clean up this mess. Where are the towels?" Tess asked.

Fifteen minutes later, after wiping up the kitchen, she suggested a video, which calmed the boys down, and then a game of checkers in the family room. They played that and several other games for the next couple of hours until Mrs. Kim came home.

"Thanks again, Tess. I'll see you on Monday, same time." She slipped two bills into Tess's hand. Tess stuffed them into her pocket and headed down the street and into her house. She didn't want Mrs. Kim to see her examining the money, even though she was eager to find out how much she had earned.

"Anyone here?" she called into the family room.

"I'm in the office, honey," her mom answered from down the hall. Tess walked into the tiny office next to her parents' bedroom. Mrs. Thomas wrote television and radio commercials and magazine ads for a big advertising agency in Los Angeles, working from her home office.

"How did it go?" she asked.

"Okay, I guess. Tyler is an angel compared to those two! Where is Tyler, anyway?"

"As usual, he is at his pal's house, Big Al. I can't wait for him to come home. He received an envelope in the mail from Robinsons-May. I think it's circus tickets. He must have won their contest. I can't imagine what else he would get from them."

"Great!" Tess said. "He's going to be psyched. Maybe he can take Big Al, too, and leave him there. He would fit right in with the clowns." Big Al was a gross, burping twerp as far as Tess was concerned. She couldn't imagine what Tyler saw in him.

"Tess, be kind. Why don't you get a jump-start on your homework? Oh, and Erin called."

"She must want to know what time we're going to the mall tomorrow," Tess said.

"We can pick her up about three-thirty. I wish you would tell me what you're looking for. Maybe I could make a suggestion."

"Um, no thanks, Mom," Tess said nervously. "I'd better start on my homework." Heading toward her room, she fished the bills out of her pocket. Fifteen dollars!

Two more jobs, and she would have earned forty-five dollars. Surely that would be enough to replace the earrings. Except, they wouldn't be the same ones. She could never really replace the important ones, the ones Grandma Kate had given Mom. Those were gone forever.

Tess sank to her knees and leaned up against her bed. What about praying? Erin's youth pastor said God knew everything about us and saw inside our hearts.

She whispered, "Dear God, Please help me replace those earrings. Please help me think before I act. I can't . . . I can't seem to do anything right. I lost my mom's earrings, and I totally embarrassed myself today in front of my science group with the papier-mâché. When will I do something right? I should probably try to fix this on my own, right? You probably have more important things on your mind, but thanks for listening. Amen."

seven

Losing Heart

Friday, October 18

"Okay, let's look at the directory and see where the jewelry stores are." Tess eagerly strode to one of the tall, three-sided mall directories. Erin followed, and the two scanned the list.

"Here's one," Erin said. "I think that's where my mom buys her watch batteries. That store must be okay. Let's go!" The two girls hurried through the mall toward the jeweler's.

"How much did you make yesterday?" Erin asked.

"Fifteen dollars. I'm going to watch the boys two more times in the next two weeks so I should make forty-five dollars. Do you think that's enough?"

"I don't know, Tess. Those earrings were awfully nice. I wish someone had found them."

"Me, too," Tess said. "Look, here we are."

The two girls rushed into the jeweler's and looked around. The glass cases shimmered, showcasing precious gems, shiny gold, polished silver, all of which rested on a bed of forest-green velour. "Why is everything always shiny and bright in the jewelry stores, but when you actually see people wearing those things they don't look the same?" Tess asked.

"I wondered that, too, so last time we were in here I asked my mom," Erin said. "Look up."

Tess did. "Wow! Check out those lights." At least a hundred light bulbs were recessed into the store's ceiling, shining majestically on the jewelry below. "Besides," Tess added, "they probably polish the jewelry every day."

"May I help you girls?" An older saleslady with half-moon glasses approached them with a certain air of disapproval.

"Yes," Tess said, "we would like to see some diamond earrings."

"Really?" The lady smiled, but the smile seemed insincere.

Annoyed now, Tess said, "Yes, I'd like to see those right there." She pointed to a pair of diamond studs nestled in the showcase, a pair about the same size as the ones she had lost. The saleslady turned to the security guard, winking before fingering the many keys on her chain. At least twenty-five keys swung from an expandable wrist band. Finding the right key, she inserted it into the small lock and reached in, sliding out the pair Tess had indicated. After briefly looking them over, Tess decided they were almost a perfect match.

"How much are they?"

The saleslady turned over the box. "Five hundred dollars."

"Five hundred dollars!" Tess shouted, shocked. "Do you have anything cheaper?" The hundred lights were bearing down on her now, pointing her out, like the floodlights of a police lineup.

"Nothing of this size or quality, I'm afraid." After replacing the gems in their velour nest, the saleslady locked up the case again. "May I help you with anything else?"

"No—no, thank you," Tess answered, stunned.

"Come on, Tess, let's get something to drink," Erin said, urging Tess out of the store. They walked a short way to the food court to order a lemonade.

After sitting there for a minute, Tess said, "Well, I'm dead. I might as well kiss my life good-bye. There is no way I can make five hundred dollars, ever. What am I going to do?" Blood rushed into Tess's face, and she blinked fast.

As Tess sniffed, Erin reached across the table to pat her friend's arm. "I wish I could help."

Tess stood up and pulled a dime out of her pocket. After walking a few steps, she threw it into the wishing well stationed in the middle of the food court. Then she came back and sat down.

"What was that all about?" Erin asked.

"I wished that the earrings would come back," Tess said.

"Wishing wells don't work, silly!" Erin said. "Have you prayed about the earrings?"

"Yes!" Tess said. "As matter of fact, I did the other night. And did anything happen? No. I don't think God answers prayers." Even as she said it, Tess knew it wasn't true, but she was angry.

"God doesn't give us a yes answer every time, Tess. Besides, don't be mad at God. You were the one who took those earrings without asking, not him. Did you only pray once? When you want something really bad, like a new bike, or to go to a movie or something, do you only ask your parents once? No! You keep asking, politely, over and over. Why don't you keep praying?"

"I suppose. I don't think God cares too much about me. I can't do anything right. I'm not special. And now," Tess sniffed, "I'm going to have to tell my mom."

"I know," Erin said. "I'll pray, too. You're my Secret Sister, right? And a sister will never let you down! I'll stick by you no matter what, even if you get in totally big trouble."

Tess reached over to squeeze her friend's hand. "Thanks. I'm glad we're friends."

Erin smiled. "Me, too."

They stood up and headed through the mall toward the front door. As they passed the stores, Tess noticed almost every one had Halloween decorations. Suddenly she stopped. In one window a cardboard skeleton waved at her. It seemed to stare right at her, with its limbs all askew.

"Remember what Jack said about skeletons?" she asked Erin.

"Yes, I do." Erin seemed surprised Tess remembered.

Standing there for a few more minutes, Tess recalled Jack saying that God sees the heart, he sees the sin there right now. Tess had taken the earrings. Tess had lost the earrings. Tess had tried to blame God for not getting them back, and God saw it all. She felt ashamed.

"Let's go," she said to Erin. "My mom will be here soon. I had better get ready to tell her. I guess I would have to tell her anyway. Even if I could have bought another pair, it wouldn't be the same pair." The two of them walked outside, leaving the skeleton behind.

eight

Confession

Friday Afternoon, October 18

"You were awfully quiet the whole way home, Tess."
Her mother looked at her. "Are you feeling okay? I
think I'd better make an appointment with Dr. Irvine.
You've had a lot of stomachaches the past couple of
months." Mom slid her keys onto the hook inside the
front door and hung her purse over a doorknob.

"Jolly good news, lassie!" Tyler zoomed through the
room waving something in the air.

"What do you have?" Tess asked.

"Circus tickets!" Tyler said gleefully.

"I thought the letter from Robinson's said someone
else won."

"Yes, but Mom and Dad decided we could go on discount family night, anyway. That's Monday. And I'm
even going to let you come!" He slid out of the tiled
hallway and into the family room, skating on his socks.

Well, now or never. "Uh, Mom, could I talk with you for a minute?"

"Sure, honey. What is it?"

"Well, can we talk in private?" Tess fidgeted, staring down at her scuffed shoe tops.

"Sure. Let's go in your room," she suggested. They walked into Tess's room and sat down on her bed.

"Well, you know how I was really nervous about going to that Harvest Party last weekend?" Tess started.

"Yes . . ."

"Well, I thought if I wore something nice, something special, I'd feel special, too."

"I thought you looked nice, Tess."

"I wanted to look even better. So, after I got out your glass-bead necklace, I searched around for a bracelet or something else." Mrs. Thomas sat quietly, and Tess gulped before continuing. "I found your velvet earring box. And when I opened it, I saw your wedding earrings. They looked so beautiful that I wanted to try them on. And when I did, I knew they would be perfect, and you weren't home to ask, but I wore them to the party anyway."

"Tess, you didn't! Those are precious to me. They should be to you, too. They'll be yours someday. But for now, they're still mine. I'm disappointed in your decision, sneaking something out of the house and then sneaking it back in. That's stealing!"

Slow tears rolled down Tess's cheeks, and the

production line sped up as her mom talked. Tess felt tiny blotches break out all over her cheeks.

"That's the problem, Mom. I didn't sneak them back in. I couldn't. When I got home and reached into my pocket to put them away—" Tess's voice broke as she sobbed out the last few words. "—they were gone!"

"Gone? What do you mean? Lost?" Her mother's face was flushed now, too. Tess knew she was angry.

"I put them in my pocket while I waited for Erin's mother to come and get us. At least, that's what I thought happened. They must have fallen out or something because, when I got home, they were gone. Erin checked in her car, and they weren't there either." She cried louder. "I didn't mean to steal them. I just wanted to look nice."

Mrs. Thomas stood up and paced around the bedroom. "Whatever got into you? Where did you get the idea that you could 'borrow' something of mine without asking? How would you feel if I sneaked into your wooden chest and took Baby Dimples out for one of my friend's daughters to play with? And then she lost her, and you never got her back?" Her mom ripped a tissue out of the box to blow her nose.

"I know it's awful, Mom. I'm so sorry. Please don't hate me." Cupping her hands over her face, Tess cried.

Finally ending her mad waltz around the room, Mrs. Thomas sat down on the bed next to Tess and reached over, pulling Tess closer. "I would never hate you, Tess.

I love you. I always will." Tess quieted some. "But I'm sad. Those earrings meant a lot to me. They were a wedding gift from my mother, and I had hoped that you, too, would wear them at your wedding."

"I know, Mom. I'm sorry. I wanted to buy some new ones for you. That's why I went to the mall." Her mother pulled Tess away from her so she could look at Tess's face. Tess wiped her hands under her puffy eyes, splashing aside the last tears. "But they cost five hundred dollars, and I only made fifteen dollars baby-sitting. I'm sorry."

Tears dripped down her mom's cheeks now, too, which made Tess start crying all over again. "I'm glad you wanted to fix the situation, Tess. But you should have come to me right away. Replacing the earrings without telling me would only have made the matter worse. It would have been lying on top of stealing." Tess's mom twisted her hands together, rubbing her wedding ring. That's what she did whenever she was agitated.

"Maybe someone will find them. Erin's mother put a note on the door at her church. So if anyone sees them, he'll call her."

"Tess, that is not going to happen. It's been a whole week. And those earrings are expensive. If someone found them, he would think it was his lucky day and keep them." She sniffed, and Tess sniffed, too. Finally she stood up. "I hope you understand the seriousness of what you have done—stealing and lying. Do you realize now how your impulsiveness will lead you to do wrong and how it can hurt others?"

"Yes, I do, Mom. I'll make it up to you, I promise."

"I think your father will want to talk with you, too. I'll call you at dinnertime." Mrs. Thomas sniffed again before pulling the door shut behind her.

An hour later, a puffy-faced, red-nosed, stuffed-up, and cried-out Tess logged into her diary.

> *Dear Diary,*
>
> *Well, I've blown it again. Now Mom knows the awful truth about her earrings, and, just like I told you, she cried. What a dope I am. Why did I take those earrings anyway?*

Tess stopped long enough to put a CD she had borrowed from Erin into the CD player. A rock rendition of "Amazing Grace" burst forth from her two small speakers. Tess put her earphones on so as not to disturb anyone.

> *Anyway, I'm going to try very hard to do some special things for my mom around the house, something good every day, like laundry or whatever. I love my mom. I feel so bad I lost her earrings.*

Tess sat quietly, thinking of how to sign off. The singer was singing about being a wretch.

> *Yes, that's me, Diary, a wretch.*

"I once was lost but now I'm found," the singer continued.

> *Am I lost, Diary? And if I am, am I worth finding?*
> *I seem to do everything wrong.*
>
> *Love, Tess*

She turned off the computer and pulled out a sheet of paper from her school notebook. She wrote in big letters: "Please do not disturb. Please leave dinner outside of door. I'll see everyone tomorrow. Love, Tess." She grabbed some tape and stuck the note to the outside of her door. There. Now they could enjoy their dinner and Tyler's plans for the circus without her ruining everything.

A few minutes later she pulled off her earphones to hear the increasingly loud knocking at her door. "Who is it?" she called.

"Dad."

Oh great, now she was really in for it. "Come in," she said, trying to be brave.

He opened the door, handing her a plate with dinner on it. "Your mother told me what happened. I want you to know how upset I am. Time and time again we have talked about how you must think before you act. This time you didn't, and look at the results." His face was red, and his head shook as he talked in a rough, barely controlled voice, sure signs of extreme anger.

"I know." Tess picked at the peas on her plate.

He sat down next to her. "Remember when you took the binoculars out of the front hall closet to look at birds? It took me a whole year to save up to buy a new pair after you dropped them. And now the earrings, which can't be replaced. Your mother and I love you, but we need to figure out what is going to get this lesson through your head. I am serious. No phone? No parties? What's it going to take?" Dad stroked the bald spot on the top of his head.

"I understand now, Dad. I really do. And I'm going to do special stuff for Mom every day to make it up to her. I promise I will think before I act from now on. I promise."

"We'll see. There will be some other discipline. I'll talk about it with Mom. Now eat your dinner and finish your homework." He squeezed her shoulder as he stood up to leave the room.

Tess watched her fish swim placidly in its algae-infested bowl. "I have to learn to think, Goldy," she said. Goldy stared back at her for a minute, then continued her laps around the bowl.

nine

Something Wonderful

Saturday, October 19

Tess could feel the gritty cleanser on her fingernails.
Her hands were tight and dry with bleach residue as
she scrubbed the bathtub, propping her knees against
its cool side. Her legs ached when she finally stood to
survey her work. There, that looked good. She had
even scraped the fungus from the rubber strips lining
the shower. Gleaming glass smiled down on her from
the mirror. Not a trace of Tyler's toothpaste spit could
be seen in the sink. Satisfied, she rinsed and dried her
hands.

Mom would surely love this. She hated cleaning the
bathrooms. What a surprise it would be when she discovered this one was done. Tess wished she could be
around to see what happened, but she liked the idea of
surprising her mom more.

"Tess, are you ready to go?" Mrs. Thomas called out
from the family room. "Dad wants to take you to Erin's

in fifteen minutes so he can come home to trim the palm trees."

Tess called back, "I'll be ready in a minute." She flipped off the bathroom light and turned toward her bedroom to change her clothes. She felt better today, being able to make up the loss of the earrings to her mother. And no matter what her mom said, Tess was going to do something wonderful for her every day this week.

Soon Tess was swiveling back and forth on the breakfast stool in Erin's kitchen. "Well, how did she take it?" Erin asked.

"I don't know. Okay, I guess. I thought she would be a lot madder, but sometimes it depends on her mood. I hate it when my mom cries. That's the worst. And, of course, she did. I know she's disappointed. She said I stole the earrings. I didn't think I was stealing them; I thought I was borrowing them . . . without asking."

"Well, you're obviously not grounded since you're here."

"Yeah, well, something worse. I was supposed to be able to start walking to the store by myself, just to Smitty's and Taco Bell. But Dad said since I wasn't making responsible decisions, I can only go with an adult."

"Oh. Sorry," Erin said. "I like going by myself. It's the only freedom I have some days."

"I know. I was looking forward to it. Oh well, he said he would reevaluate in a few months." Tess looked as if she might cry again. Then she brightened. "But I am making it up to my mom, doing special stuff for her every day this week. Like today I cleaned the bathroom."

"I folded all the laundry last time I sassed my mother," Erin said. "I think she was glad I knew I had done something wrong." Erin pulled some lunch meat and mayonnaise out of the refrigerator. "Do you want cheese on your sandwich?" she asked.

"Okay," Tess answered. "If you have orange cheese. I don't like white cheese."

"Me either. That's so weird, like we really *are* sisters! Will you grab the bag of chips out of the cupboard behind you?" Erin finished making the sandwiches and put them into a picnic basket. "Do we want a blanket?"

"Yeah, that would be fun."

"Okay," Erin said, "I'll get one." A few seconds later she returned with a ragged purple blanket. "It's sort of old, but at least my mom won't care if it gets a little dirty." The two of them headed out into Erin's backyard. "Was that your dad who dropped you off?"

"Yeah," Tess answered.

"I wish my dad were home on Saturdays," Erin lamented. "He's gone a lot. But he is trying to figure out how he can spend more time at home. He says the restaurant falls apart when he's not there. As the head chef, he doesn't trust the other chefs to do everything like he does."

They spread out their blanket under a gnarled pecan

tree. "If we pick up some of the nut shells, this would be a good place to sit," Erin said.

"Did I tell you we're going to the circus Monday?" Tess asked.

"How fun! Your brother won those tickets?"

"No, but my parents knew how much he wanted to go; so they bought tickets for discount family night this Monday. I guess we'll go after I baby-sit."

"Are you still baby-sitting? I mean, now that you can't buy your mom the earrings?" Erin asked.

"Yeah, this coming Monday; also next week, if she needs me. It's really sort of fun. And the money is good."

"I bet. I wish someone would ask me to baby-sit! What are you going to do with the money?"

"I don't know," Tess answered. She took a bite of her sandwich, chewed for a moment, and said, "Remember last Saturday night when Jack said God sees sin in our hearts?"

Erin finished her chip. "Yes."

"Well, I—I'm not sure I know what sin is. Is it stealing? Or killing people? Or what? I don't think I'm really bad even if I do make some mistakes," Tess finished.

"The Bible says all people sin, which is just making wrong choices. Doing something other than what God wants for them, whether they meant to do it or not," Erin said. "I'm not sure where it says that, or the exact words, actually." Her cheeks turned valentine red. "Bible memory is my worst thing. I don't practice very much. I wish I were better. But I can look it up or ask my brother and tell you next week."

"No, don't ask your brother. I'd be sort of embarrassed if he knew I didn't know what it was," Tess said.

"Maybe I can ask my Sunday school teacher," Erin offered.

"Okay."

"Do you want to come to church with me tomorrow?"

"No, thanks," Tess said. She peeled her orange and popped a section in her mouth. After swallowing she continued, "I think I'll do the laundry for my mom, then I have to write my fairy tale. Do you know what you're going to write yet?"

"No, I can't think of anything. I want it to be good. And I won't have too much time to write. Tomorrow is church, and tomorrow night we're going back because it's missionary night."

"You go to church on Sunday nights, too? Isn't that a lot? Don't you get sick of it?"

"I do get bored sometimes," Erin said. "But we don't go every Sunday night. And I know I won't be bored this Sunday night because the missionaries tell stories about the cool places they live and about the people they live with. And they show slides."

"Oh," Tess said, "it does sound fun." She wrapped her orange peel in her napkin before plopping it into the basket. "I guess I won't be having fun anymore." Tess picked at her sandwich crust and looked toward the ground.

"Don't worry, Tess. It will turn out all right. I'm sure your mom thinks you're more important than any earrings. And you have me, right? We're sisters. Let's change the subject and think of some fun stuff to do together. I've been thinking about a few things."

"Yeah?" Tess looked up, smiling at last. "Like what?"

"Well," Erin continued, "since we're almost the same size, what if I put together an outfit for you from my clothes, and you put one together for me out of your clothes. We'll meet in the bathroom before first bell."

"Okay, then what?"

"Then we change clothes! We really have to trust the other person not to pick out something dorky for us to wear."

"Cool. Let's do it! How about Tuesday, since we're going to the circus Monday night?"

"Okay," Erin answered. They swapped Secret Sister bracelets to close the deal, which they always did to seal a promise. Tess popped the last bite of sandwich into her mouth, already planning what Erin would wear.

ten

Three-Ring Circus

Monday, October 21

"No way," Tess said, hands on hips and mouth pursed. "You guys are not fixing another snack by yourselves. Remember the peanut butter cocoons hanging from the wallpaper last time I was here? I'll help you."

Tess marched the two Kim boys into the kitchen and found a bag of microwave popcorn. While waiting for the popping to stop, she mixed up a can of juice. She then poured some melted butter on the popcorn, and the three of them walked back to the family room.

"Do you want to play checkers?" Jerry asked.

"Sure, where's the board?" Tess asked.

"Under the TV cabinet. Joe, get it out."

Joe crawled across the carpet and pulled the checkerboard out from under the TV.

"I get to go first since I got the board out," Joe whined.

"All right. Don't be such a baby." Jerry crammed

another handful of buttery popcorn into his mouth. "Ongwy don taktoo yong," he said through his stuffed mouth. After swallowing, Jerry said, "I'm going to wash this slimy butter off my hands while you guys play." Pushing himself to his feet, he ambled toward the kitchen.

Tess and Joe moved their pieces around the board and through the squares until Tess won. "Hey, you're bigger so you're supposed to let me win!" Joe whined. "Besides, my mom is paying you."

"She's paying me to baby-sit you, not to let you win," Tess said. "What's taking Jerry so long?"

"I'll go see." Joe stood up and headed for the kitchen.

Tess grabbed the remote control and flipped through the channels for a minute. She paused on an advertisement for "Miracle Cream, the beauty dream for skin so soft your man will beam."

Hmm, Tess thought, *my mom writes better ads than that. They should hire her, and they would sell more. Hey, maybe Erin and I could sell stuff. We would make way more money than baby-sitting, and I could still buy something nice for Mom.*

"Knock it off!"

A shout interrupted her thoughts, and she ran to the kitchen. As soon as she entered, a spray of water shot across the room, nailing her in the face. "You guys, turn that water off right now."

Jerry aimed one last squirt at Joe's face with the

sink's nozzle attachment before twisting the cold water off. Tess headed toward him; he tried to escape her grasp and fell flat on the floor, slipping on a puddle.

"Ouch!" he bawled.

Joe laughed. "Serves you right; you started it!"

"Guys, guys." Tess tried to calm everyone down. "Are you okay?"

The boys nodded glumly, refusing to look at each other.

"Here, let's clean up." Ripping several sheets of paper towels off the rack, Tess handed the wad to Joe. "Start mopping."

Jerry smirked. Tess tore off more paper towels. "You, too," she said, handing the second wad to Jerry.

A few minutes later the kitchen looked tiptop again, and the boys watched a video until Mrs. Kim came home.

After Mrs. Kim paid her, Tess ran to her waiting family. "Thank goodness you're here!" Tess said to her dad as she climbed into the car. "That job is work! I'm happy to be leaving to go to the real circus, although it seems like one in there."

"Most jobs are work, Tess," Dad said with a smile. "What happened?"

"They had a water fight, and we had to mop up the whole kitchen. But I earned another fifteen dollars; so now I have thirty dollars."

"What are you going to do with it?" her mom asked

as she twisted the rearview mirror toward herself to fix a contact.

"I can't see what's behind me," Tess's dad grumbled. He always grumbled when she took the mirror.

"Now, dear, I'm already done," she said, twisting the mirror back. "Well, Tess, what are you going to buy?"

"I don't know. I saw an ad today for some Miracle Cream."

"Miracle Cream! That's dumb," Tyler said. "I'd buy something cool, like Lizard Village or a Scotland Yard trench coat. It's not fair. Girls can baby-sit to make money, but boys can't do anything! Dad says I'm too young to mow lawns, and there's nothing else to do." He crossed his arms for emphasis.

"You have the rest of your life to work, Ty," their dad teased.

"And boys can baby-sit," Mrs. Thomas added.

"I didn't say I was going to buy Miracle Cream!" Tess interjected. "I was just going to tell Mom I thought she could write a better ad. This one was goofy."

"Thank you, Tess," said her mom. "I'll keep it in mind. Now, let's all help Dad look for a good parking spot." After five minutes spent circling the arena, she finally spied a spot, and Mr. Thomas pulled the car in.

"I'm so excited! I can hardly believe it! This is the best day of my life!" Tyler practically leaped out of the car and started to walk toward the arena door.

"Wait up, Ty," their dad said. "This is a busy street. We need to walk across together."

Once inside the arena, they climbed row after row of stairs until they reached their seats. "My dad would say we were two rows from heaven when we sat this high up," Mrs. Thomas joked.

Tess looked up. She wondered if heaven was that close. Sometimes she thought it was, but sometimes it seemed very far away.

Darkness fell across the room, and the circus started. Neon necklaces that had been hawked by the walking vendors flashed color strips here and there through the inky black. Men in tall hats stationed themselves around the crowd like the royal guard, steadying stacked trays of Sno-Kones and popcorn and peddling furry tigers at "exorbitant prices," according to Mr. Thomas. A roar swelled from the crowd as clown after painted clown paraded around the ring, followed by bejeweled elephants and exotic women. Tigers with shiny orange coats and saber-toothed grins leaped about the center ring.

The first act was the flying trapeze artists, some with safety ropes, some without. Their white sequined costumes reflected the strobe light, making the performers look like angels flitting through the air unaided. Soon after their act ended, the roar of metallic engines filled the great hall and was so loud Tess covered her ears. Thick exhaust fumes rose to their seats, clinging to the air around them as the daredevil motorcyclists entered the Globe of Death. Unbelievably, they circled one another again and again, three motorcycles riding at high speed inside a wire globe.

In awe, Tyler elbowed Tess. "Have you ever seen anything so great?" He was so excited he forgot his British accent.

"Actually, Tyler, I think the whole circus is pretty cool," Tess whispered back. "I'm glad you wanted to come."

After an hour, intermission was announced, and the lights flashed on.

"Let's get a soda," Mr. Thomas suggested. The four of them began the long descent down to the snack-bar area. On the way Tyler discovered a booth selling mini Globes of Death and ran over to them, pulling his family along. Small motorcycles rode around the inside of the globe, a perfect replica of the show they had just seen.

"Can I get one? Please, please?" he asked.

Mom shook her head. "They're twelve dollars, Tyler. That's too much."

Dad nodded in agreement. "I don't mind paying for the tickets, but extras are your responsibility. Don't you have any allowance saved up?"

"Nah." Tyler shook his head, looking dejected. "I spent it."

As they started to walk away, Tess tugged on her mother's arm, stopping her. "Wait a second." Tess fumbled in her pocket until she pulled out two neatly folded bills, the ones Mrs. Kim had used to pay her a couple of hours before. "Here, Tyler, you can have this," she said.

"Are you serious?" Tyler stared at her with disbelief.

Tess nodded her head, then stuffed the bills into his hand. "Quick, get one before they sell out."

"Thanks, Tess. You're the best sister in the whole world!" Tyler gave her a high-five then hopped over to the sales booth with his mother.

Mr. Thomas pulled Tess toward him, hugging her against his side as he did. "That was very generous, Tess. I know how hard you worked for that money."

"Yeah, well, it's okay," Tess said. She was happy she could use the money to buy something nice for her brother, even if she couldn't buy new earrings for her mom. And maybe her parents would notice how responsible she was acting, sharing and all. She and her dad slowly strolled toward the refreshment stand to order sodas before the show resumed.

eleven

Bull's-Eye

Tuesday, October 22

"How was the circus last night?" Erin called over the bathroom stall as she struggled to zip up the top Tess had brought for her to wear.

"It was totally fun. I liked the trapeze the best. Tyler liked the Globe of Death, and Mom liked the tigers. Dad said he liked the popcorn best, but he was joking. I think he liked the flame eaters. What size is this, anyway?" Tess sucked in her stomach and buttoned the jeans. She fluffed the shirt over her waistline and dug into the bottom of the brown bag for accessories.

"Doesn't it fit?" Erin asked. "This is great. I love beads. I didn't know you had a bead necklace."

"Yeah, my cousin sends me jewelry every year for Christmas. Sometimes it's good; sometimes it's not. Last year, she hit a winner."

"Back to the circus," Erin said. "They ate flames?"

"Yeah, it was weird. I've always been afraid of fire; so it was pretty scary just to watch."

The girls came out of the stalls at almost the same time. "Ta da!" Erin said, twirling so Tess could see the warm peach top, the beaded necklace, and the khaki pants. "What do you think?"

"It looks a lot better on you than on me," Tess said. "And what do you think about my wardrobe?" she teased.

"Great. I knew it was you!" Erin said admiringly. Tess wore a pair of Erin's black jeans and a kitten-soft, light-weight white sweater. "White isn't so good on me. But with your long, dark hair, it's just right."

Well, that's a first, Tess thought. *My hair is good for something!*

The bathroom door squeaked open, and Tess and Erin turned to see who was coming in. Colleen, Tess's one-time best friend, and her partner in crime, Lauren, strutted into the bathroom. Colleen stared coolly at Tess, then whispered something in Lauren's ear. Lauren looked back and laughed, then headed into a stall. Tess felt chilled and was glad Erin was there. Tess and Erin gathered their things into the brown paper sacks and were just ready to leave when Lauren came out to wash her hands. Lauren glared into the mirror with an "I'm great and you're bait" look.

"Hey, Lauren," Erin said.

"Yes?" Lauren answered, in a how-dare-you-talk-to-me voice.

"I'd take the toilet paper off of my backpack before I went into class, if I were you," Erin said. Then she and Tess headed toward the door. Tess sneaked a peek as she walked out and saw Lauren plucking two squares of wet toilet paper from the back of her pack.

Once in their classroom, Erin said, giggling, "Some things never change."

"It's true." Tess nodded in agreement. How could she ever have wanted to be like Colleen and Lauren? How could she have thought Colleen was her friend? After Colleen had burned Tess last month, she knew the truth. And now she had Erin, a true friend and a sister.

"Let's never be like that," Tess said.

"I agree," Erin answered. Tess took off her bracelet to swap with Erin, to seal the deal.

A few hours later, at lunch, Erin waved her hand in front of Tess to get her attention. "Yoo-hoo, are you here?"

"Yeah, yeah, I'm here."

"Isn't that great about Ms. M? I was so proud of my brave sister. You must have gotten all the courage genes!" Erin said.

"What's so brave about asking her?" Tess asked. "Do you think she will invite us to the wedding?"

"The whole class? I don't know. Maybe they wouldn't all want to go. Like Joann, for instance." Erin stood up. "Come on. Let's go outside."

Tess gladly agreed. They walked past the boys' table,

and Tess noticed Erin blush as she glanced at Scott Shearin. Hmm, she would have to ask Erin about that later.

The weather was cooler now, and a thoughtful breeze blew out summer, ushering in the desert fall. A few leaves, wet from the sprinklers, stuck to the playground fence like soggy Wheaties to the side of a cereal bowl. Autumn in Arizona was like a second spring, and people spent more time outside.

The two girls walked to a corner of the school and sat down against the outer brick wall. Erin crossed one leg over the other.

"Remember when you asked me the other day what sin was? Well, I had a chance to talk with my Sunday school teacher about it. She drew me a picture, like this." Erin pulled out a piece of notebook paper and drew a big circle, then a smaller circle inside it, then a smaller circle inside that. It looked like a bull's-eye.

"I used to think sin was only really bad things, like murder or something. But my teacher explained that the word sin means 'missing the mark,' like in target practice or darts, when you don't hit the center. Anything except the exact center, doing exactly right, is sin. She wrote down this verse for me to show to you." Erin fished a piece of paper out of her pocket, smoothing the folds as she opened it and handed it to Tess.

Tess read, " 'If we say that we have no sin, we are fooling ourselves, and the truth is not in us. But if we

confess our sins, he will forgive our sins. We can trust
God. He does what is right. He will make us clean from
all the wrongs we have done'—1 John 1:8-9."

Erin chewed on her pencil before taking the piece of
paper back from Tess and scrawling, " 'God makes
people right with himself through their faith in Jesus
Christ. This is true for all who believe in Christ, because all are the same'—Romans 3:22."

"Do you get it?" Erin asked.

"Yeah. That's really good that you memorized that
last one. What do '1 John 1:8' and 'Romans 3:22' mean?"

"That's where you can find them in the Bible. So you
know it's from God, not something some person made
up." Erin beamed. "Thanks for the compliment. About
memorizing, I mean. I did it for you." She fingered her
French braid in embarrassment.

Tess smoothed out the paper and picked at the
ragged edges while looking at the bull's-eye. Dropping
little paper scraps in a pile next to her, she said, "I
guess I missed the mark with those earrings."

"It's okay. God knows we make mistakes. That's why
it's so great that as soon as we tell him we're sorry, he
forgives us. So we don't have to walk around feeling
bad or guilty all the time. When God forgives our sins,
he throws them as far as east is from west."

"Wow, that's pretty far!"

"I know."

"So, is that what being a Christian is?"

"What do you mean?"

"Just memorizing the Bible and doing what it says?"

"No, silly." Erin punched Tess's arm. "You ask his forgiveness for your sins, and you trust him to take charge of your life. That's the 'believing' part I just read."

Tess sat quietly, thinking about how she had tried to blame God at the mall for not finding the earrings. She guessed that was missing the mark, too. "Still, I don't think there's anything so great about me that God would want to forgive me, even though I would like him to throw the earring mess as far as east is from west."

"God thinks you're great, Tess, and so do I. You're the only sister I've ever had."

"Thanks. But I don't want to talk about this anymore, okay? We only have a few minutes left before class. Let's go on the bars." Tess stuffed the paper into her jeans pocket, and they joined some of the girls from their class in a chasing game.

911

Wednesday, October 23

Tess walked up to her house, flipped open the mailbox at the end of her driveway, and sifted through the mail. "Why do I do this? There's never anything for me."

She shuffled through the catalogs and bills and looked at contests and coupons for carpet cleaning. Then a curious pink envelope caught her eye. It was addressed to: Tess Thomas, 225 Foothills Manor Drive, Scottsdale, Arizona. The return address was: You'll Never Guess, 1000 Secrets Lane, Sistersville, AZ.

"Who could this be from?" she wondered, ripping open the envelope.

Tess slipped a pretty pink note card from the envelope and read, "Roses are red, but my sister is blue. I want you to know that I'm praying for you." Tess smiled and put the card back into the envelope. What a good friend. And praying couldn't hurt, right?

She set her backpack on the floor and hummed to

herself as she pulled a package of chicken pieces out of the refrigerator. This, she thought, would be the ultimate gift to her mother during her week of trying to do really wonderful things. Her mom would forgive her for the earrings for sure now. Poking her fingernail through the plastic wrapping, she heard a little "pop" as the wrap snapped.

"Now, what am I supposed to dip this stuff into?" Thumbing through her mom's big cookbook, she found a recipe for fried chicken and read, "Put flour, salt, and pepper in a medium-sized bowl. Dip chicken pieces in raw egg then dredge in flour mix. Fry pieces until golden brown."

Molly Thomas loved fried chicken, and Tess wanted to make sure she prepared it just right for her mother. Tess had never actually fried anything before, but it couldn't be too hard. After dipping the chicken in the egg and then the flour, she put the pieces in a pan with a large amount of oil. Then Tess washed her hands, and taking a head of lettuce and several tomatoes out of the refrigerator, she turned her attention to the salad.

"What are you doing?" Tyler and Big Al walked into the kitchen.

"Making dinner."

"Blimey. Does Mom know?"

"No, silly. It's a surprise. She's going to be back from the dentist's office in a few minutes, and I wanted to have this done so she could relax."

Big Al opened his mouth, propelling a huge belch

from the yawning hole. Suddenly the smell of rotten hot dogs filled the room.

"That was totally disgusting. You guys get out of here."

"Come on, Tyler. Let's go throw the ball." Laughing, the two of them headed out to the front yard to toss a baseball around. Tess turned back to the salad.

Funny, that burp must have been worse than she had thought because now it smelled smoky. Her noise twitched as the awful smell grew stronger. Tess twirled around and saw swirls of black smoke rising from the frying pan. Splatters of oil popped out of the pan onto the stovetop, and she could see the oil smoking more and more.

"Oh, no. Now what?" She grasped the panhandle but recoiled as the heat burned her hand. "Where is the potholder?" She searched frantically as the smoke grew thicker. The splattering reached the floor now. Still unable to locate the potholders, she grabbed a dishtowel and grabbed the handle again.

As she picked up the pan, the towel rested a moment too long on the heating element. Suddenly the entire towel caught fire, racing up to Tess's hand. "Ouch, ouch, ouch!" she cried, throwing the burning towel. Almost instantly the small garbage can in which the towel landed caught fire. "What should I do?" she cried aloud. Running to the telephone she quickly dialed 911.

"911. Fire, police, or ambulance?" The operator spoke in a too-calm voice.

"Please help. I've started my house on fire!" Tess shouted into the receiver.

"Is anyone else in the house?"

"No, my brother and his friend are outside. Everyone else is gone. Please get someone here quickly!" Tess screamed.

"Okay, miss, your address popped up on our screen; someone is on the way. Go out of the house to flag down the fire trucks." Tess tried to hang up the phone, but her hands were shaking so hard she dropped the receiver and flew out the door.

Her voice trembled as she screamed, "Tyler!"

Tyler and Big Al took one look at her face and ran to her side. "What's the matter?" Tyler asked.

"The house is on fire, the house is on fire!" Tess cried.

"What do you mean?" Big Al asked.

"It's on fire! Please, God, let the fire trucks get here." In a moment the sad wail of sirens could be heard several streets away.

Tyler's eyes grew as big as an owl's. "Are you okay? What happened? Boy, are you going to be in trouble."

Tess knew the fire trucks were almost there, but the waiting seemed unbearable. Suddenly, the trucks turned the corner, and the three kids flailed their arms wildly to get the firefighters' attention. Two big trucks, a pumper truck and a hook and ladder, pulled up. A large man in yellow and gray reflective turn-out gear jumped off the truck and ran up to Tess while two other firefighters hauled a hose toward the house.

"Is anyone in the house, miss?" he asked in a kind voice.

"No, no, everyone's out here."

"Where are your parents?"

"My dad is at work, and my mom is at the dentist. She'll be back soon." At that thought, Tess started to cry again.

"Don't worry, young lady. We'll take care of everything." The firefighter sent the three of them to wait by the curb while he joined his partners at the front of the house. He sent someone over to look at Tess's hand.

"This is a nasty burn, miss. You need to get this taken care of right away. Here, wrap this cold pack around it. It will lessen the pain for about half an hour. By then, you should have some medical treatment." The firefighter wrapped a cool, blue quilted bandage with icy water between its layers around Tess's hand. He was right; it did soothe the throbbing hand a little bit. But it still hurt, bad. Where was Mom?

A few minutes later her car came barreling down the street. It screeched to a halt in front of the house. Tess could read the fear in her mother's face as she viewed the fire trucks, then the relief as she saw the three of them out front.

"What's going on? Is everyone okay?" she asked Tess.

"Mom, I'm so sorry. I wanted to make you fried chicken, and I grabbed the pan with a dishtowel, but it caught on fire. The next thing I knew the garbage can was on fire; so I called 911."

Tess started to cry all over again. Tyler and Big Al stood dumbfounded, watching the firefighters. Tess's mom hugged her. A few minutes later the captain signaled for Mrs. Thomas to come over.

Tess waited by the curb, but she could hear him. "Everything is okay. There is minor damage to one wall, and the curtains are burned. It's mostly cosmetic, nothing unsafe, but it will be a shock at first. Your daughter's hand could use some medical attention. I don't think it's too bad. I didn't want to call an ambulance and scare her further. A doctor should see her, though."

"Thank you," her mom said. "I'll take her to the emergency room right away."

The firefighters packed up their gear, and the two trucks rolled down the street back to the firehouse. Tess's mom walked slowly back to her. "My goodness, my goodness, whatever will we tell Jim?" she muttered to herself. After glancing at Tess's face, she added, "Don't worry, honey. Accidents happen. Let's go to the emergency room to take care of your hand. We'll talk about this later." She went into the house to survey the damage and to call her husband. A minute later she came back out to the front yard.

Tess sobbed as she climbed into the car, but she slowly calmed down. "Let's take Al home on the way," her mother suggested. Tyler nodded his head, and the two boys got into the car. Mrs. Thomas looked at Tess's throbbing red skin, adjusted the cool wrap, and stepped on the gas. Tess stared out the window the whole way to the hospital, jiggling her hand up and down in her lap to distract her from the pain.

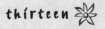

thirteen

Making Things Right

Wednesday Evening, October 23

"Wait in here, please. The doctor will be just a minute."
The nurse pulled the door shut, leaving Tess and her
mother alone in the room. Tyler had decided to wait at
Big Al's until Mr. Thomas could pick him up.

"Tell me what happened, Tess," her mom said gently.

"Just what I said, Mom. I wanted to make some fried
chicken for you. You know, to do something really nice
like I've been trying to do all week. I thought if I made
your favorite dinner, then you could relax when you got
home, and you would totally forgive me for losing your
earrings. Only the oil started to smoke, and when I
tried to take the pan off the stove, the towel caught fire.
When it burned my hand, I threw the towel, and it
landed in the garbage can. I called 911 and ran outside." Tess sat quietly.

"I know it was an accident. I appreciate that you were
trying to do something nice for me, Tess. But I told you

the other day, you don't have to do anything else to make up for the lost earrings. I forgive you; I understand that people make mistakes. 'Forgive' means I am 'giving' you the gift of forgetting the wrong. You don't earn it; it's a gift. That's what the 'give' part of the word means. So please don't do anything else to try to make it up to me." Her eyes twinkled. "Especially frying chicken!"

"Don't worry about that! I'm never cooking again, or at least not for a few years!" Tess promised. The door swung open.

"Let's see that hand, young lady," the doctor said as she entered the room. She shook hands with Tess's mom. "I'm Dr. Norton." Gently turning Tess's hand and lower arm, the doctor examined the burn. "I don't think it's too serious. Let's put some medicated ointment on it and wrap it in gauze." She sprayed Tess's skin with a cool mist. "That's to deaden the pain while I spread the cream." Then she spread some thick white cream on the burned area and rewrapped it in a fresh bandage.

"You should stay home from school for a couple of days to avoid infections or bumping the healing tissue. Have your regular doctor check it on Friday. What's your doctor's name? I'll have my nurse call to make the appointment for you."

"I'll come with you so we can find a time that will work for both of us," her mom said. "Will you be okay?" she asked Tess.

"Yes, Mom, nothing to burn down in here," Tess joked. "And the skin does feel better with that stuff on it." For the first time since she had burned her hand, Tess could move it without too much pain.

Dr. Norton and her mother left the room, and Tess looked around her. A blood pressure machine with its black air hoses was screwed into the wall. A scary-looking cabinet had a sign attached to it that read "Oxygen Tent." Kicking her feet against the back of the table she sat on, Tess examined the chart over the sink. "The Skeletal System," it read. It was more detailed than the skeleton in the mall, with lots of blue and red veins woven alongside pink muscles. Not a Halloween decoration, but a skeleton nonetheless.

"God, do you see my heart? If you can see my heart, you know I meant to do something good this time."

The door swung open again, and the nurse came in with some information on caring for burns. Then she sent Tess out to the waiting room. "Your mom is waiting for you. I gave her the instructions," the nurse said.

"Thank you," Tess said.

Mrs. Thomas picked up her purse and put her arm around Tess, guiding her to the car in the dusky evening light. Two squirrels scurried through the parking lot, seeking walnuts under the trees. Tess smiled at their chatter, and her mom smiled, too.

✳

"Is Erin there?" Tess rested against her propped-up pillows, trying hard to ignore the smell in her house. It reminded her of a campfire that had been doused.

"Hello?"

"Hi, this is Tess."

"I know who you are, silly. How are you?"

"Not so good, actually," Tess said. "I started my house on fire and had to go to the hospital."

"What?!" Erin shouted into the phone. "Are you okay?"

"Yeah, I got a little burned, but I'm okay, and so is everyone else. The house isn't even too bad, if you ignore the smell. It's a long story; I'll tell you more later. What I really wanted to know is if you could bring my assignments to my house tomorrow. I have to stay home for two days until the bandages get changed on my hand."

"Sure, Tess. I'm sorry you'll miss school tomorrow. We're going to read our stories and have popcorn and stuff."

"I know," lamented Tess. "But there's nothing I can do about it. Hey, thanks for the card! I really loved it."

"You're welcome. I hope it made you feel better. Plus, I always like to get mail."

"Me, too," Tess said, "and I never do." After a quiet moment she continued, "I saw a skeleton at the hospital."

"A skeleton?" Erin asked.

"Yeah. And I was wondering, do you think God loves me enough to forgive me? My mom said she forgives me, but she's my mom."

"Yes, Tess, he does. I wish you could hear my story tomorrow. I heard it at missionary night last Sunday and liked it so much I chose it for my project."

"Yeah, well, maybe you can bring it over when you bring my other homework." A few seconds passed in silence. "I'd better go. My hand hurts."

"Okay. Bye, Tess. I'll pray for you." Erin said.

"Thanks." Tess gently hung up the phone then walked to her closet. Picking up the white jeans she wore yesterday, she pulled out the pocket, searching for the piece of paper Erin had given her. She laughed. Last time she was looking in these pockets it was for the earrings. She hoped the paper wasn't lost. She found it and opened it up.

"God makes people right with himself through their faith in Jesus Christ," she read. Hmm. Not from doing good stuff all the time, or being skinny or popular or smart. Or never making mistakes.

But what did "faith" mean? That was sort of a new word. Hopping off her bed, Tess found her dictionary and looked up the word. "Confident belief in and trust in someone or something," the dictionary said. Did she have confident belief in and trust in Jesus Christ?

After clicking off her light, she folded up the piece of paper and stared out her window. Mr. and Mrs. Cricket were there, chirping cheerfully. Goldy swam round and round her slimy bowl, getting in her exercise.

"Tomorrow," Tess promised herself, "I'll clean off the slime." She snuggled down in her bed and tried to sleep.

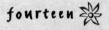

fourteen

Twenty-One Ponies

Thursday Night, October 24

"Erin's here," Tyler shouted as he knocked on Tess's bedroom door.

"Will you send her in?"

"Okay."

A few seconds later Erin appeared at Tess's doorway. "Hi. How are you feeling?"

"Okay. My hand feels much better today."

"Could I see where the fire was?"

"Sure." Tess closed her book and hopped off her bed. She slipped her feet into her warm wool slippers and adjusted her sweatshirt. "Come on. I'll tell you all about it on the way."

"Man, this still looks pretty ugly," Erin said.

"I know. My mom is going to buy some new curtains, and my dad is going to paint the wall. I think it will look okay then."

A few minutes later, after they had walked back down

the hall into Tess's room, she said, "How was school today?"

"Totally fun. I'm sorry you had to miss it. Ms. M. made popcorn and brought chocolate and fruit punch."

Tess smiled. Leave it to Erin to tell her about the food first. "How did the stories go?"

"Great. They were pretty good. I can't believe how well some of those guys can write. People you would never guess, like Angela and Steven."

"How did yours go?" Tess asked.

"Fine. Everyone liked my story, too. I told them it was a missionary story but didn't say the whole comparison. I wrote it on the bottom of the page, though, so you can read it."

"What do you mean, the whole comparison?"

"You'll see when you read it," Erin said. "Hey, before I forget, here are your assignments." She dumped a pile of books onto Tess's bed and handed her a folder full of papers. "Ms. M. wrote out all the instructions for both today and tomorrow. I told her you would be back Monday, right?" Erin asked.

"Yep, that's right. Hey, what's that?" Pulling a large piece of orange construction paper from the stack, Tess opened it up to its full size.

"We made you a card. Everyone signed it."

Tess smiled, looking it over. "Was this your idea?"

"No, um, actually . . ." Erin seemed embarrassed. "Believe it or not, it was Joann's."

Joann! Tess never would have guessed. Reading the

comments, she cracked up when she got to Scott Shearin's. It read, "If you were going to burn some place down, why not the school?" Everyone had written something or drawn smiley faces or hearts. Erin signed it, "Your Secret Sister" and someone else had scribbled, "What?" next to that. Tess opened her desk drawer and pulled out a roll of Scotch tape, then stuck the card to her wall.

"Thanks for bringing everything over, Erin." Tess hugged her.

"No problem. It's what any sister would do. I'll miss you tomorrow. Oh, here are your clothes. My mom was, um, a little upset that we changed clothes at school. She thought maybe we should only switch clothes at home from now on."

"Okay. Sounds fine."

"Yeah, I'd better go. My dad is waiting." Erin beamed. "He took the night off."

"Great. I'll call you tomorrow night to find out what happened in class."

After Erin left, Tess shut the door and kicked off her slippers. She sifted through the stack on her bed, opening the manila envelope marked "Twenty-One Ponies." *This must be Erin's story.* She pulled the sheets of paper from the envelope and settled back on her bed to read.

Twenty-One Ponies
Long, long ago on the dusty prairie of the wild west, a tribe of native Americans lived, a large tribe

with many traditions and customs. The old people of this tribe told the stories of their past so the young people would never forget. One particularly old woman, named Rock by the Bank, told the best stories. Because she had only three teeth you had to listen closely to understand her words. Her favorite story went like this:

One year the most eligible young brave in the village grew to be the age that men are when they choose a bride. Each day he sat outside his tent, watching the young women of the tribe. One girl was the most beautiful. Her long black braids hung down her back, reflecting the summer light. Her skin was as smooth as a stone on the bottom of a quick-moving stream. Another girl was wise. She taught the others how to weave and how to braid detailed patterns. Another girl knew the best places to find tasty berries and roots. Whoever married this girl would certainly eat well. None of these women stirred his heart.

One day his attention was drawn to a shy young woman who normally stood to the side of the others. This young woman, named Forget Me Not, was not particularly beautiful nor did she weave beautiful bracelets or headbands. The first morning he observed her she brushed the mud off the moccasins of the others who had kicked them off in their haste to get to the river. That same afternoon she comforted the crying baby of a new mother, enabling the mother to prepare the evening meal. Although Forget Me Not's singing voice was not particularly good, the brave noticed that, when the woman laughed, all those around her laughed, too. Her joy was contagious. He decided he wanted that joy in his household.

According to the custom of his people, he approached the girl's father. "I would like your daughter's hand in marriage," he said. "What will her bride-price be?"

"This one is not beautiful, nor does she know where to find hidden fruit. I think one pony will be enough," the father answered.

The brave and the father shook hands, and the young man agreed to come back the next week to claim his bride. That night he peeked outside as the village girls giggled. "One pony isn't much," one said. "Of course, Forget Me Not isn't a valuable bride."

"That's true," another one chimed in. "My betrothed promised three horses for me!"

The brave closed his teepee to think. The next morning he came to me, Rock by the Bank, and asked, "What is the biggest dowry paid by any man in the history of our tribe?"

I told him, "Legend says that twenty ponies were paid for Prairie Thorn's hand in marriage in my grandmother's years." The brave thanked me, then went home.

That week he rounded up his seventeen horses, all but his favorite. He traded some fine beaten silver to another brave for two more ponies and a large sack of grain for another. Finally, he walked out to where his horses stood. His favorite, the one he had raised since birth, stood outside the crowd.

This pony was special, unblemished, unbroken to the ways of the world. The brave loved this pony more than anything else in the world; it was more valuable to him than all his other possessions combined. After kissing the pony's coat, he led him with all the others to his new father-in-law's house. As the ponies beat a path to the door, the entire village gathered around, wondering why there was a stampede.

"Here I am," the brave called. "Come to collect my bride."

The father-in-law answered, "But I said one pony was enough."

"No," said the brave. "My bride is worth more than all others in the entire history of our tribe. Here are twenty-one ponies, including my favorite."

Forget Me Not walked out of the tent to join her new husband, holding her head high before all those who had made fun of her. For the rest of her life she knew her husband prized her enough to give up all he had for her, not for what she had to offer, but because she herself was loved.

Tess noticed that Erin had scribbled at the bottom of the page, "So you see, Tess, this is really the story about God, the brave, and his love for his bride, you. He gave everything he had for you, including that which he loves the most, Jesus Christ. Not because you do anything great, but because he loves you exactly as you are. That's why he will forgive you, and you can trust him with your whole life. Isn't this a neat story? I heard it last Sunday night."

❋

Tess walked into the silent kitchen and squeaked open the patio door. The evening was light on her skin, the breeze soothing her as it lifted up her hair. The pool cleaner wandered on its nightly rounds. As she watched the cleaner, Tess wiped two small tears off her cheek and reclined in a worn-out woven lawn chair and looked up toward heaven. "Yes, God, I understand," she whispered. "You do want me and love me. I'm sorry for taking the earrings and then blaming you. And for all the other times I missed the mark." She lay there for another minute.

"I don't know if I said everything right, or what I'm supposed to do after this. Please forgive me. I want things to be right between us. Erin said being a Christian is asking for forgiveness and having faith in Jesus. I asked for your forgiveness, and the dictionary says faith means believing in and trusting. So I guess I'm saying, I do trust you. Starting now, I'm yours. I don't really know what to do next, though, so you'll have to tell me."

She didn't hear a voice, but almost immediately she felt peace and joy wrap around her like the fuzzy pink blanket that Baby Dimples, her doll, snuggled in. Even though the night was dark and starry, Tess felt warm, as if she had climbed out of a chilly pool into the strong summer sunshine. In some way, Tess felt as if she had been underwater for a long time and only now could she deeply draw in some fresh air and really breathe.

fifteen

Real Sisters

Friday, October 25

"Isn't it great how fast my hand is healing?" Tess asked. "I'm glad I can go to school Monday. I want to be there when we blow the volcano."

"Yes, honey, it really is great." Her dad pulled the car into the driveway. "Mom will be pleased to see the bandages are off." He stopped the motor, and they got out of the car. "I'm going to do a little work in the garage. Why don't you go tell Mom you're home?"

"Okay." Tess walked into the kitchen. "Here I am. No bandages! Dr. Irvine says my hand looks good."

"I'm glad," said her mother. "Why don't you help me make some dinner?"

Her mom's face sported a huge smile. She must have had a fantastic day. But why was she flinging her hair around? Every time she turned around, her hair swung away from the sides of her face. Weird. Tess turned back to the sink.

"Notice anything?" asked her mom.

"Uh, let's see." Tess stared. Not new clothes or shoes. "New makeup?" she guessed hopefully.

"No, silly, look!" She swept back her hair again. There, like twin twinkling stars, were the diamond wedding earrings, one clinging for dear life to each ear.

"Mom! Where did they come from?" The carrot scraper dropped in the sink as Tess rushed over to hug her mother. "Oh, Mom, I'm so happy!"

"Me, too, honey. While you and Dad were at the doctor's office, Erin stopped by with these. I guess the church landscaper found them in the bushes next to the driveway, where you must have dropped them. When he pruned the bushes, they practically called out to him. After he took them to the church office, the secretary called Erin's mom, who picked them up. She and Erin rushed right over here. Oh, Tess," she said, "isn't this wonderful?"

"Yeah, it's been a great week! I'm going to go call Erin and thank her." Skipping out of the kitchen, Tess headed to her room. She picked up the phone to dial, then set it down.

"Lord," she started, remembering that Erin's family called God "Lord," "Thank you for the earrings. You got them back for me after all!" Pausing for a moment, she added, "Even though you forgave me anyway!" Grabbing the phone again, she dialed Erin's number.

"Hello?"

"Great job!" Tess shouted into the phone. "I am so excited I can barely even talk!"

"I know. I couldn't believe it myself! My mom and I practically laughed the whole way to pick them up."

"Guess what else?" Tess asked.

"What?"

"I loved your story. And I understood it! Last night I prayed to thank God for loving me, for thinking I'm valuable just as I am, and for forgiving me. I told him I trust Jesus now."

"That's great! This is one of the best days of my life. I can't believe it!"

"Why not?"

"I don't know. It seems so fantastic. God answered my prayer and yours, too. It's too dreamy to be true. But it is true! Do you know what else?" Erin asked.

"What?"

"Well, now we're not just Secret Sisters, we're real sisters, spiritual sisters."

"What does that mean?"

"Well, since God is our father, Christians call other Christians their sisters and brothers. So now you're really my sister."

"Does that mean Tom is my brother?" Tess giggled.

"I guess so. Hey, what did your mom and dad say?"

The room was silent for what seemed like ten minutes, although it was probably less than one. "Tess? Are you still there?"

"Yes."

"Well, what do your mom and dad think?"

"I haven't told them yet. I guess I will later."

"Oh. Okay. I'd better go, I hear my mom calling us for dinner. We can talk more tomorrow, all right?"

"Okay, Sis. See you later." Tess hung up the phone and sat heavily on her bed. She had forgotten about telling her parents. Somehow she thought her mom wouldn't mind, but she knew dad wasn't into religion. This wasn't just religion, but would he see it that way? Maybe she would tell them next week, after she had thought about a good way to say it.

She glanced at the orange card on her wall, reminding her how much the class cared for her. On the spur of the moment, she pulled out her top desk drawer and grabbed a snapshot of her and Erin riding horses at Erin's party last month. She taped it to the wall next to the card.

"I hope we're Secret Sisters forever," she whispered, heading back to the kitchen.

Have More Fun!!

Visit the official website at:
www.secretsisters.com

There are lots of cool activities, exciting things to do with
your own secret sisters, games, updates, a photo gallery,
and other great stuff. Be the first to know when new
books are released! See you there today!

If you would like to write to me, please send mail to:

Sandra Byrd
P.O. Box 2115
Gresham, OR 97030

Special Delivery

Everyone likes to get mail, and your secret sister is no exception! Putting together a special correspondence file makes it easy for you to surprise her with mail.

You need:

1 folder with pockets on each inside flap
4 sheets of paper or blank cards
4 envelopes
Stickers
4 stamps

Pick a time of the week, for example, Sunday night, to write your sister a little letter. It can be a rhyming poem or a coded message or just a few words about how exceptional she is. Decorate it with your stickers and markers or pretty hole punchers if you like. Fold it and stamp it and stick it into your mailbox before you go to bed. Your sis will get a Tuesday surprise, and might even write you back!

Can you guess what happens in Star Light, Book 3?
Solve this puzzle, and see what it is to be!

Across

5 Horned toad
7 Faith
9 Animal friends
10 Another word for
   "vomit"
11 The kind of trip
   you take with
   your class

Down

1 The opposite of
   life
2 Creamy, cold
   snack in a cone
3 Sickness
4 Baby meow
6 Twinklers
8 Planet home
11 A good time

**Look for the other titles in
Sandra Byrd's Secret Sisters Series!
Available at your local Christian bookstore**

Available Now:

#1 *Heart to Heart:* When the exclusive Coronado Club invites Tess Thomas to join, she thinks she'll do anything to belong—until she finds out just how much is required.

#2 *Twenty-One Ponies:* There are plenty of surprises—and problems—in store for Tess. But a Native American tale teaches her just how much God loves her.

#3 *Star Light:* Tess's mother becomes seriously ill, and Tess's new faith is tested. Can she trust God with the big things as well as the small?

#4 *Accidental Angel:* Tess and Erin have great plans for their craft-fair earnings. But after their first big fight will they still want to spend it together? And how does Tess become the "accidental" angel?

#5 *Double Dare:* A game of "truth or dare" leaves Tess feeling like she doesn't measure up. Will making the gymnastics team prove she can excel?

#6 *War Paint:* Tess must choose between running for Miss Coronado and entering the school mural-painting contest with Erin. There are big opportunities—and a big blowout with the Coronado Club.

#7 *Holiday Hero:* This could be the best Spring Break ever— or the worst. Tess's brother, Tyler, is saved from disaster, but can the sisters rescue themselves from even bigger problems?

#8 *Petal Power:* Ms. Martinez is the most beautiful bride in the world, and the sisters are there to help her get married. When trouble strikes her honeymoon plans, Tess and Erin must find a way to help save them.

The Secret Sister Handbook: 101 Cool Ideas for You and Your Best Friend! It's fun to read about Tess and Erin and just as fun to do things with your own Secret Sister! This book is jam-packed with great things for you to do together all year long.

Available March 2000:

#9 *First Place:* The Coronado Club insists Tess won't be able to hike across the Grand Canyon and plans to tell the whole sixth grade about it at Outdoor School. Tess looks confident but worries in silence, not wanting to share the secret that could lead to disaster.

#10 *Camp Cowgirl:* The Secret Sisters are ready for an awesome summer camp at a Tucson horse ranch, until something—and someone—interferes. What happens if your best friend wants other friends, and you're not sure but you might too?

Available September 2000:

#11 *Picture Perfect:* Tess and Erin sign up for modeling school—and get their first assignment! But when they show up, they find out that things aren't always what we expect, a fact confirmed when Tess's mother has her baby.

#12 *Indian Summer:* When Tess and Erin sign up to go on their first mission trip—to the Navajo reservation—they plan to teach vacation Bible school. As often happens, they end up learning more than they teach, and Tess has the most important experience of her new Christian life.